Creative Kids
publishing

ISBN 978-1-55454-447-9

Copyright © 2008 Creative Kids Publishing, a division of
Transglobal Communications Group, Inc.
5550 Skylane Boulevard, Suite G
Santa Rosa, CA 95403

The Gingerbread Man

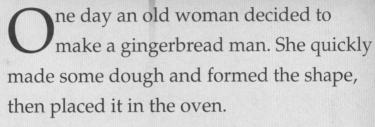

One day an old woman decided to make a gingerbread man. She quickly made some dough and formed the shape, then placed it in the oven.

While the cookie was baking, a voice suddenly shouted from the oven. "Let me out!" it cried.

The old woman open the door and out jumped the little gingerbread man. He sang as he ran across the floor and out the door:

"Run, run, as fast as you can,
You can't catch me,
I'm the Gingerbread Man!"

The old woman ran after the Gingerbread Man, but could not catch him.

She stopped at her doorway and stood yelling after the Gingerbread Man, "Come back. Come back!" But the Gingerbread Man just kept on running.

The Gingerbread Man ran and ran and ran. He ran faster and faster until, finally, he ran as fast as he could.

"I'm faster than anybody or anything," he thought to himself proudly.

The Gingerbread Man continued down the path which crossed through a field. There, he met a cow grazing.

"Stop, little man!" said the cow. "You look very good to eat."

The Gingerbread Man ran faster as he sang out:

"Run, run, as fast as you can,
You can't catch me,
I'm the Gingerbread Man!"

The cow chased after him, but the Gingerbread Man was too fast.

Further down the road, the Gingerbread Man came across a hungry horse. "Stop, little man!" the horse called. But the Gingerbread Man only sang as he ran even faster:

"*Run, run, as fast as you can,*
You can't catch me,
I'm the Gingerbread Man!"

The horse galloped and galloped, but soon tired and could not catch him.

The Gingerbread Man was quite pleased with himself. He decided to take a rest beside a nearby tree.

Minutes later, the Gingerbread Man resumed his run. Soon, he met a fox.

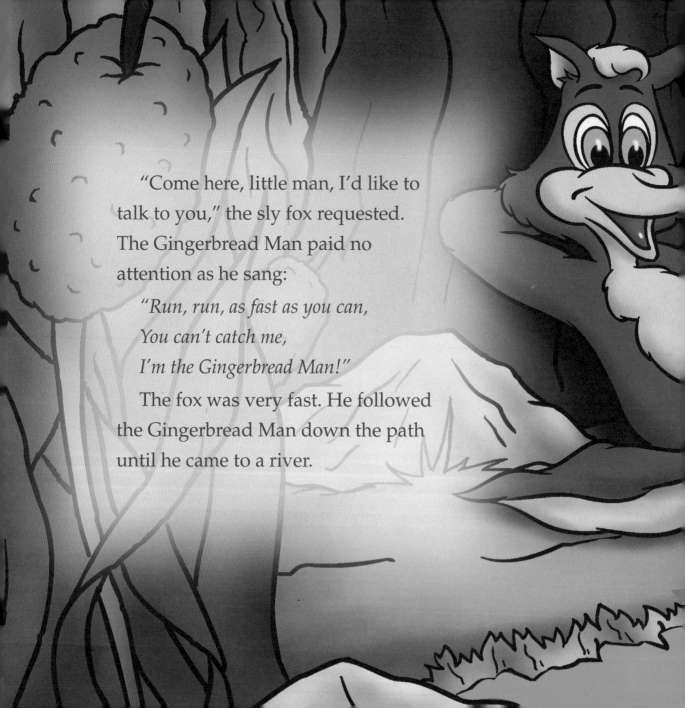

"Come here, little man, I'd like to talk to you," the sly fox requested. The Gingerbread Man paid no attention as he sang:

"Run, run, as fast as you can,
You can't catch me,
I'm the Gingerbread Man!"

The fox was very fast. He followed the Gingerbread Man down the path until he came to a river.

"If you ride on my tail, I'll take you safely across the water," the fox told the Gingerbread Man. He climbed onto the fox's tail. They began to swim across the river.

"You're too heavy for my tail. Jump onto my back," said the fox. So, onto the fox's back the Gingerbread Man jumped.

The fox swam a little further. "You're too heavy for my back. Jump onto my nose!" demanded the sly fox.

The Gingerbread Man began to feel afraid. Still, he moved onto the fox's nose.